Shirley Barber's
FAIRY
Stories

SUMMIT
PRESS

CONTENTS

•

•

SUMMIT PRESS

Published by
Summit Press Pty Ltd
950 Stud Road, Rowville
Victoria 3178 Australia
Phone: +61 3 8756 5500
Email: publishing@fivemile.com.au

This edition first published 2002
Reprinted 2003, 2004

Copyright © Marbit Pty Ltd
Text and illustrations by Shirley Barber
Cover design by Sonia Dixon
All rights reserved

Printed in Hong Kong

ISBN 1 86503 781 8

National Library of Australia Cataloguing-in-Publication data

Barber, Shirley
Shirley Barber's fairy stories.

For children
1. Fairies – Juvenile fiction. 2. Unicorns – Juvenile fiction. 1. Title.
A823.3

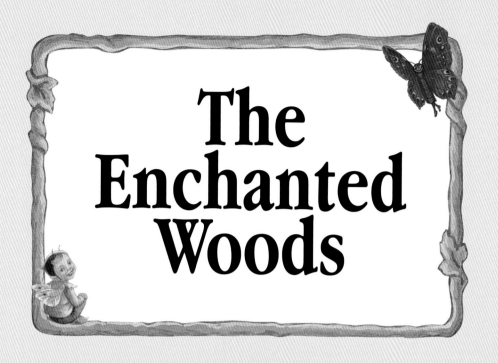

The Enchanted Woods

Words & pictures by Shirley Barber

One warm, sunny day, Sarah Jane
wandered into the woods to play
with her toys and look for wild strawberries.

But when she stopped to play under a tree, she had a strange feeling she was being watched…

Then, to her surprise, she glimpsed a procession of fairies winding through the trees. Some were quaint and impish, and others were the most beautiful creatures she had ever seen.

She followed them as they made their way deep into the woods.

Eventually, they came to a big old tree, and under the tree was a ring of mushrooms.

It was a magic fairy ring. But Sarah Jane didn't see it until after she had stepped inside. She stared at it, puzzled, and wondered what it was.

Suddenly, the fairies ran out from behind the trees and began to laugh and dance around her.

"Sarah Jane," they cried, "you are needed in Fairyland. Now that we've caught you in our fairy ring, we can take you with us!"

Then they waved their magic wands, and Sarah Jane felt herself become smaller and smaller.

She was now no taller than the fairies, and felt as light as thistledown. The fairies took her gently by the hands, and together they flew up above the tree tops and out over a shimmering sea.

They landed on the shores of a strange and beautiful land. The flowers were taller than they were, and huge butterflies waited to greet them.

Soon, a messenger arrived from the fairy palace.

"Sarah Jane," he announced, "the fairy King and Queen have been told of your arrival, and they would like to see you now."

So the fairies sat Sarah Jane on the back of a butterfly, and together they flew over a lake and towards the fairy palace.

The King and Queen welcomed Sarah Jane, and told her why she was needed in Fairyland.

"Our daughter is to be married to a prince from a neighbouring kingdom" said the Queen. "We need the presence of a mortal to ensure their good fortune and a happy marriage."

"Yes," said the King. "You will bring them good luck."

Soon, it was time for the wedding.
The chatter and laughter of the guests grew
quiet as they gathered to watch the Prince
and Princess exchange their wedding vows.

After the wedding, a magnificent banquet was held in the glittering hall overlooking the lake. Everyone, including Sarah Jane, feasted on the finest delicacies Fairyland had to offer.

When the banquet was over, it was time for the Prince and Princess to leave. Together, they descended the golden stairway, as their guests cheered and showered them with rose petals.

They were carried away to their new home in a beautiful carriage drawn by a flight of dragonflies.

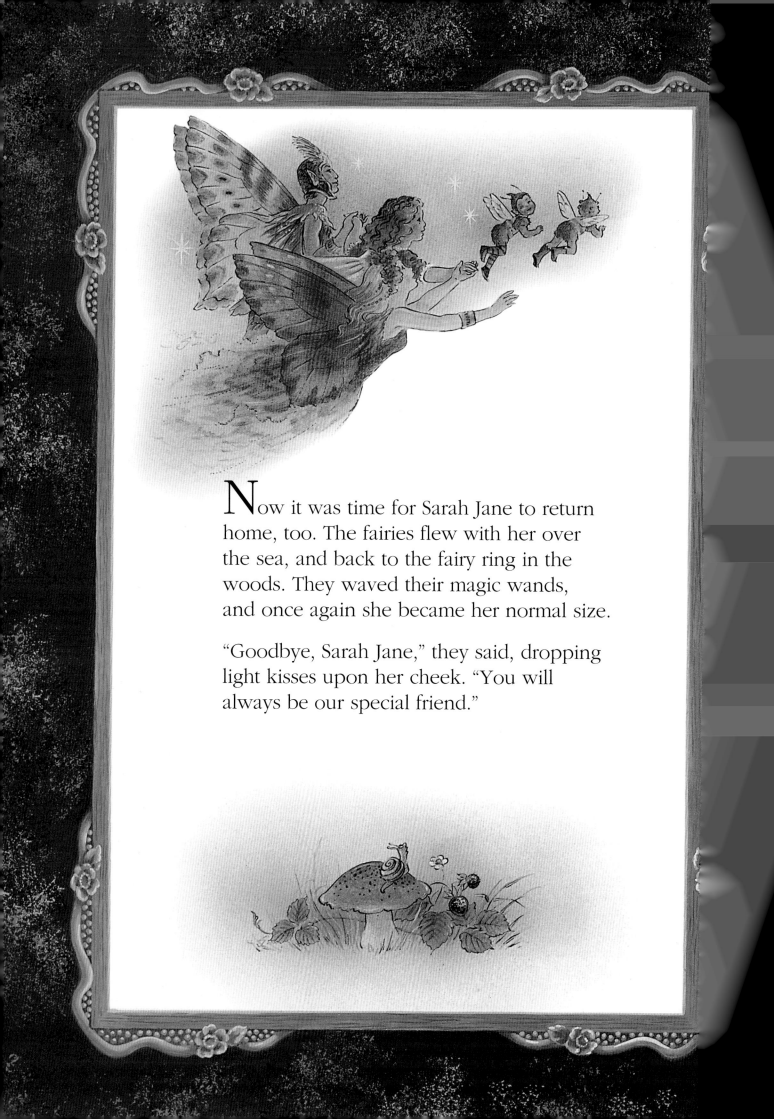

Now it was time for Sarah Jane to return home, too. The fairies flew with her over the sea, and back to the fairy ring in the woods. They waved their magic wands, and once again she became her normal size.

"Goodbye, Sarah Jane," they said, dropping light kisses upon her cheek. "You will always be our special friend."

Sarah Jane picked up her basket and toys and wandered home. She had nothing to show for her adventure but, to her family's surprise, her basket was now overflowing with small, delicious strawberries. They were a gift to her from the fairies, a sign to show she really *had* been to Fairyland.

THE SEVENTH
UNICORN

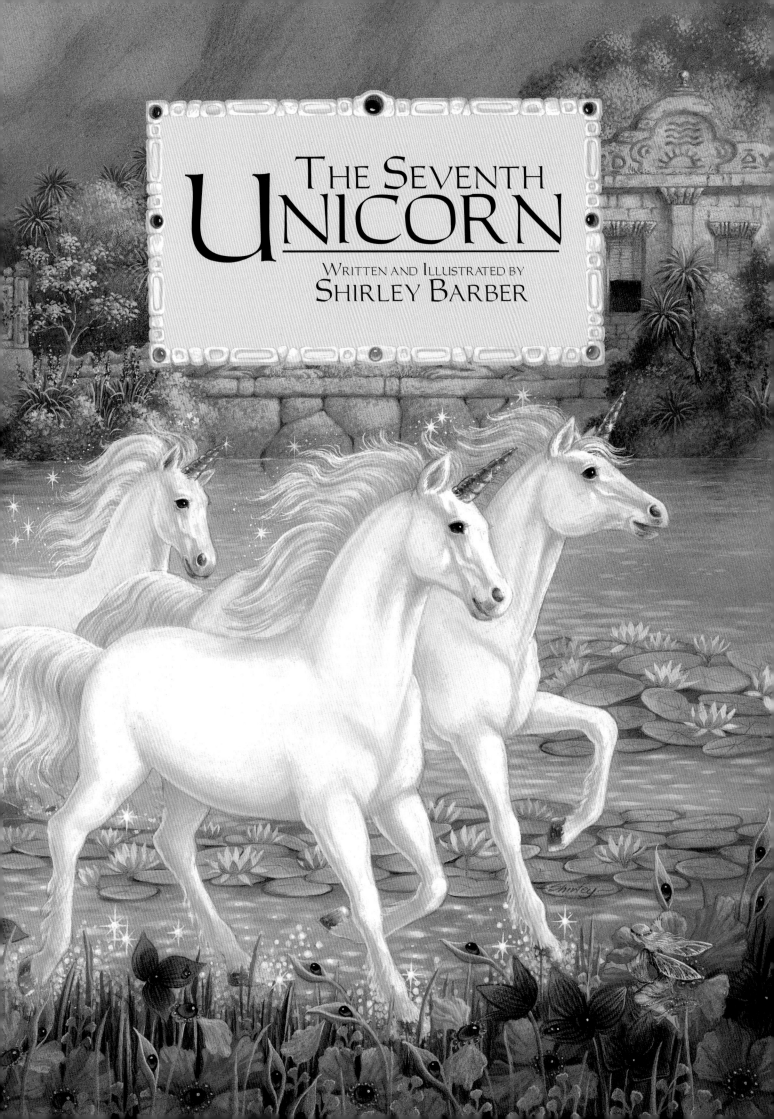

The Seventh
Unicorn

Written and Illustrated by
Shirley Barber

$\mathcal{O}$ak Avenue was a narrow tree-lined street in the oldest part of a large city. Shaded by the oak trees were tall old-fashioned houses, many with high-walled yards between them where horses and carriages had once been kept.

In more recent times, the ground floors of most of the houses had been turned into quaint-looking shops. Robert and Rachel often came to stay with their Aunt Zelda, who lived above her gift shop.

Many of the shops in Oak Avenue had names
that were easy to remember. Aunt Zelda's gift shop
was called The Magic Mirror because the first
thing you saw, right at the entrance, was a big
mirror in a strangely-carved frame. The mirror was
so old that the glass was misty and silver-speckled.
Rachel felt sure it really *was* a magic mirror.

"If you gaze into it for a long time you begin to see
a beautiful world in there, behind the silver
speckles," she said.

Robert just laughed and Aunt Zelda, closing the
barred shop door, replied, "You might see it more
clearly if you gave the mirror a good polish."

So early next morning, when the avenue was quiet
and no one was about, the children polished the mirror.

Robert was impatient to try
out a new giant slide which had been
set up in the park at the end of Oak Avenue.
So when they had finished cleaning the mirror he
ran off. Rachel was about to follow him when a
sudden movement made her glance back at the
mirror. Imagine her amazement when she saw a little
pearl-white horse leap from the mirror in a swirl of
star-dust, and trot swiftly away between the trees.
"A unicorn!" she whispered. "I'm sure it was a
real-live unicorn!"

THE MAGIC MIRRO

Rachel ran to catch up to Robert.

"Oh, come on, Rachel," he scoffed, "First a magic mirror and now a unicorn!" With that he dashed into a corner store to buy a bag of his favourite barley-sugar twists. Rachel stood crossly looking at the gemstones in Jemima's Jewels shop window.

"I really did see a unicorn," she thought to herself.

But when Robert reappeared and gave her some barley-sugar she stopped feeling annoyed with him, and the two raced off to the park together. The giant slide was such fun that Rachel almost forgot about what she had seen until...

...the little white
unicorn trotted into view! His
horn and hooves were golden and
star-dust glittered in his mane and tail.
He came right up to the children, as if he
wanted to play. "What did I tell you?"
Rachel whispered. "Isn't he beautiful!"
"Yes! And he absolutely loves
barley-sugar!" laughed
Robert.

The honking of a distant car-horn startled the
unicorn and he suddenly wheeled in a cloud of
star-dust and galloped away, his golden hooves
silent on the fallen leaves.

"Let's go back and tell Aunt Zelda that her mirror
really *is* magic!" said Rachel. So the children
hurried back along Oak Avenue, but this time on
the other side. As they were passing the high-
walled yard next to The Wizard's Castle, an
antique shop, Robert stopped suddenly.

"What is it?" asked Rachel. Without replying,
Robert scrambled up the nearest oak tree and
peered over the wall. "Rachel," he called down
softly. "There are six more unicorns in there.
They're all tied up, and they look very unhappy."

"Come down quickly!" hissed Rachel. "Someone's coming!" Down slid Robert, just in time.

A man had unlocked the shop door and was carrying out a strange assortment of antiques to arrange on the pavement. He wore a wizard's pointed hat with the name of his shop on it, and a big cloak sewn with stars, so that he looked just like a real wizard. When he went back into the shop the children sped past and up the avenue towards Aunt Zelda's gift shop.

The children were almost at Aunt Zelda's shop
when the seventh unicorn cantered past. Right
before their eyes, he leapt back into the mirror.

"Come on!" cried Robert. "Follow him!" Despite his sister's protest, Robert pulled her with him into the mirror, and they went through the glass as if it was water.

On the other side of the
mirror Rachel's nervousness
faded as she saw they had
entered a beautiful land,
strangely shadowed at the
edges but filled with
jewelled flowers
and grasses.

"Welcome to Arcadia," said a soft voice
behind them. Rachel and Robert turned
and saw a group of beautiful children.
"Or welcome to what is left of Arcadia,"
said their leader. "For see how on every
side a shadow creeps to destroy
our lovely world!"

Rachel and Robert looked
where the girl pointed. They
realised that what they had thought was a
shadow was really a creeping fog which
withered flowers and trees where it touched them.
"An evil wizard discovered the spell to open a door
into our world," continued the young Arcadian leader.
"Each day he entered through the magic mirror, bound
a unicorn with a magic halter and led it away. When he
steals our last unicorn, Arcadia will be destroyed —
only the power of seven unicorns keeps our world
whole and well. We sent our seventh unicorn
through the mirror to seek out the other six
but he could not find them."

Rachel and Robert looked at each other. *They* knew where the missing unicorns were. The wizard must have entered the magic mirror while Aunt Zelda was at the back of the shop.

The children quickly jumped through the magic mirror into the shop. Excitedly they told their amazed aunt all that had happened.

"We must work out a plan to rescue the other unicorns," she said, once she had recovered from her surprise. "We'll have to start very early in the morning before the wizard is out of bed — and we'll need a big bag of barley-sugar!"

Next morning at sunrise,
while Aunt Zelda guarded the Magic
Mirror doorway, Rachel and Robert ran down
Oak Avenue. Rachel kept a lookout for the wizard
while Robert climbed over the wall to where the
unicorns huddled miserably together. He quietly
unbolted the big gate and pulled off the magic halters,
one by one. The six unicorns silently trotted out
into the street, where Rachel gave them each
some barley-sugar. Soon the two children were
running full speed up the avenue with
the hungry unicorns following
close behind.

Aunt Zelda was anxiously waiting outside her gift shop, ready to guide the unicorns back to Arcadia. Rachel leapt through the mirror, ahead of the unicorns, and threw handfuls of barley-sugar among the jewelled flowers. The six unicorns followed her back into their own world, and began to crunch the barley-sugar.

Next came Robert and Aunt Zelda.
With cries of joy the Arcadians came
running to hug and pet their unicorns,
all seven together again at last.
Then, golden light filled the
land and the dark shadows
were driven away.

For a moment they stood watching,
then Aunt Zelda drew the children
back to their own
world...

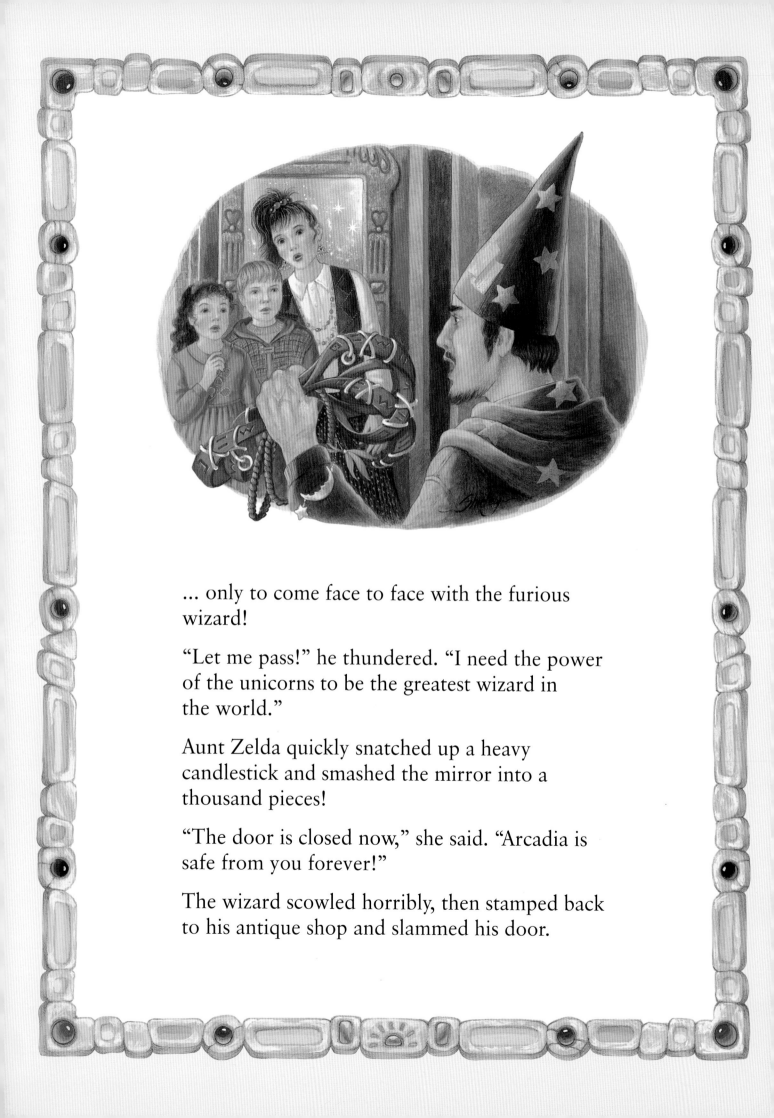

... only to come face to face with the furious wizard!

"Let me pass!" he thundered. "I need the power of the unicorns to be the greatest wizard in the world."

Aunt Zelda quickly snatched up a heavy candlestick and smashed the mirror into a thousand pieces!

"The door is closed now," she said. "Arcadia is safe from you forever!"

The wizard scowled horribly, then stamped back to his antique shop and slammed his door.

Aunt Zelda and the children were overjoyed that they had saved Arcadia from the wizard. They knew they would never forget that beautiful world as long as they lived. The ornate mirror frame was soon fitted with a new glass, and although it was no longer a doorway into another world, Rachel and Robert often gazed into it. Sometimes they could just make out a shimmering pearly form. They were sure it was a unicorn looking out at them — perhaps he was thinking about barley-sugar!

Shirley Barber's
SPELLBOUND
A Fairytale Romance

Shirley Barber's
SPELLBOUND
A Fairytale Romance

$\mathcal{O}$nce upon a time some fairy folk lived in a little town
by a sparkling stream. Their tiny houses were built among
mossy boulders, half hidden by drooping ferns. The fairy
King and Queen lived with their two daughters in a palace
made of leaves and petals and with vine-clad balconies
overlooking the water.

Princess Rowena was dark-eyed and raven-haired, and
little Lisette was the fairest of all the golden fairies.
But Princess Lisette was so sweet-natured and so lovely
to look upon that Princess Rowena, though equally
beautiful, became troubled by envy and deeply unhappy.

The King was kept busy with the affairs of his kingdom,
and the Queen by her younger children, so neither
noticed their daughter's unhappiness.

*P*rincess Rowena was some years older
than Princess Lisette, and had helped to care for her as a
child. But as the little golden fairy grew into a beautiful
young girl, so too did the envy grow in her elder sister.

Princess Rowena had found she was able to cast spells,
which was a rare and valued gift among her people. She
knew she should never misuse her gift to harm others,
but gradually her envy overcame her better feelings. She
ordered a golden armlet to be made, and as the jewels
were set in it she imbued it with a powerful spell.

One evening, Rowena gave her sister
the magic armlet. Lisette exclaimed with delight as its
jewels sparkled in the lamplight. "I shall always wear it,
dear Rowena," she promised, as she slid it upon her
arm. "It is so sweet of you, but then, you have always
been such a kind sister to me."

Rowena went to stand for a while on
the balcony and gazed down at the moonlit water. She
knew that while her beautiful sister was bound by the
spell in the armlet she would become tired and unable to
fly as a fairy should. The envy within her was satisfied,
but her heart was heavy for she knew she had
done a great wrong.

 ow, in a neighbouring kingdom, two
handsome princes were bidding farewell to their
father and mother in an airy palace suspended
between pink and white foxglove spires. They
were about to set out on a journey to find two
fairy brides.

"Choose wisely," commanded King Aven. "They
must be of royal blood, and beautiful, if possible, for
the sake of our people —"

"— and sweet-natured," put in Queen Bel, "so that I
may find it easy to love them."

"Healthy and strong," continued the King, "for they
must fly with you and help you to care for the fairy
people in your kingdom. Remember, Burnet, this
kingdom among the foxgloves shall be yours one
day, and you, Trefoil, shall have the meadowsweet
realm on the banks of the stream."

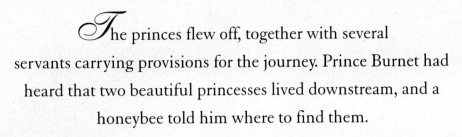

The princes flew off, together with several
servants carrying provisions for the journey. Prince Burnet had
heard that two beautiful princesses lived downstream, and a
honeybee told him where to find them.

"They live downstream among the ferns," he buzzed.
"I z-z-zee them when I fly down for a drink of water."

At nightfall, the princes arrived at King Azolla's palace. A fanfare of honeysuckle trumpets announced them.

King Azolla and Queen Bryony welcomed them and introduced their daughters. Young Prince Trefoil had no sooner set eyes upon the golden-haired Princess Lisette than his heart was hers forever, while Prince Burnet fell quickly in love with the raven-haired Rowena.

Later, Prince Burnet said to his brother, "I would look no further for my bride than Princess Rowena except that I feel something is wrong here. There is a strange power in the elder sister and a strange weakness in the other. Perhaps I should look elsewhere for my bride."

"But I have found mine," declared Prince Trefoil. "I shall ask Princess Lisette to be my bride."

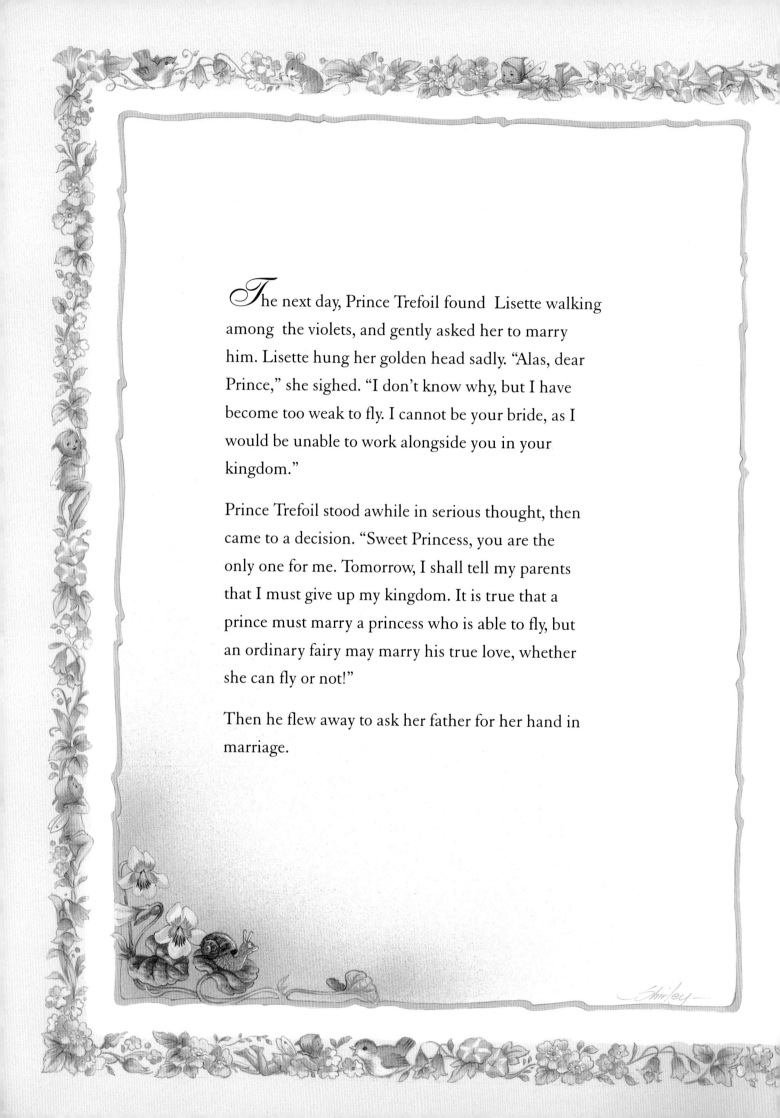

The next day, Prince Trefoil found Lisette walking among the violets, and gently asked her to marry him. Lisette hung her golden head sadly. "Alas, dear Prince," she sighed. "I don't know why, but I have become too weak to fly. I cannot be your bride, as I would be unable to work alongside you in your kingdom."

Prince Trefoil stood awhile in serious thought, then came to a decision. "Sweet Princess, you are the only one for me. Tomorrow, I shall tell my parents that I must give up my kingdom. It is true that a prince must marry a princess who is able to fly, but an ordinary fairy may marry his true love, whether she can fly or not!"

Then he flew away to ask her father for her hand in marriage.

Once he was out of sight,
Princess Lisette shed bitter tears.
"I cannot let my dear Prince ruin his life for me,"
she sobbed. "I shall go far away where he can't find me.
Then perhaps he will forget me and marry
another fairy who can fly."

She walked out over the floating leaves of
water plants and stepped into a fallen leaf. She pushed
it into the middle of the stream where the fast-flowing
current carried her swiftly down the valley.

Meanwhile, King Azolla and the two princes spent much time in anxious talk. The King praised Trefoil for the strength of his love, but said he must not give up his kingdom without consulting his parents.

Suddenly, word came that Princess Lisette was missing. They all joined in the search for her, but she was nowhere to be found.

After several days of searching, all hope of finding her was gone, but the heart-broken Prince Trefoil announced he would keep looking until he found her. Nothing his brother or the King and Queen said could make him change his mind, and he flew away alone, down the valley into wild regions where no fairies had ventured before.

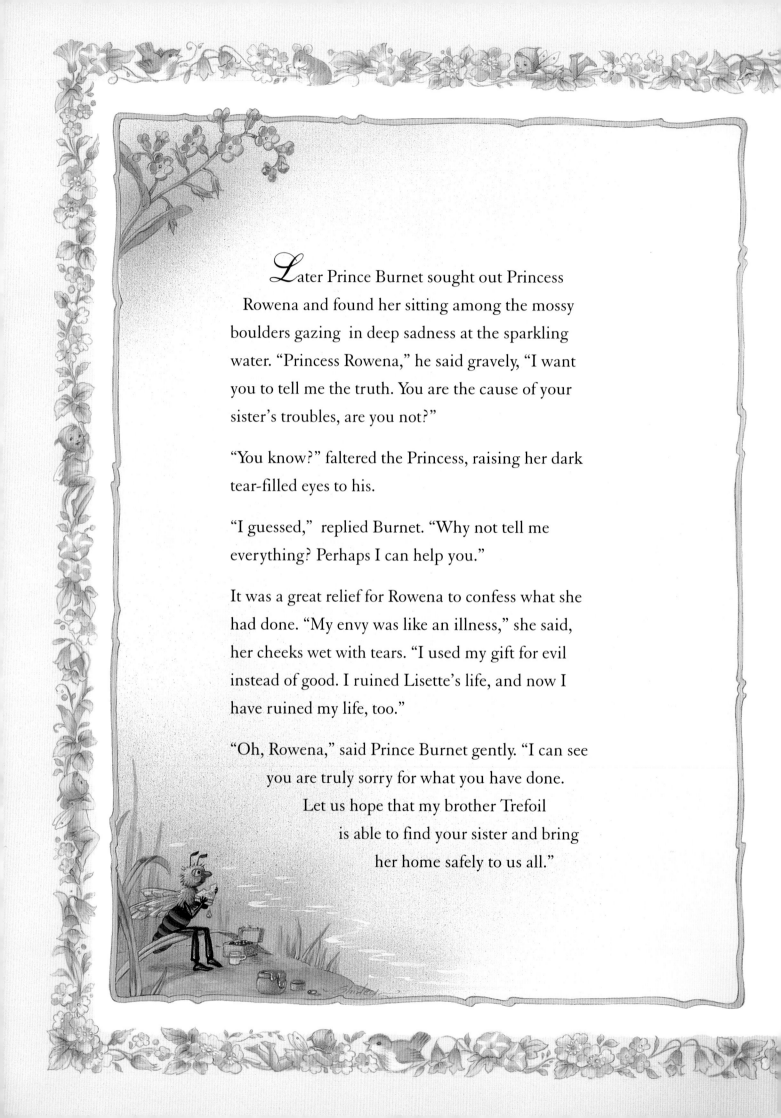

$\mathcal{L}$ater Prince Burnet sought out Princess Rowena and found her sitting among the mossy boulders gazing in deep sadness at the sparkling water. "Princess Rowena," he said gravely, "I want you to tell me the truth. You are the cause of your sister's troubles, are you not?"

"You know?" faltered the Princess, raising her dark tear-filled eyes to his.

"I guessed," replied Burnet. "Why not tell me everything? Perhaps I can help you."

It was a great relief for Rowena to confess what she had done. "My envy was like an illness," she said, her cheeks wet with tears. "I used my gift for evil instead of good. I ruined Lisette's life, and now I have ruined my life, too."

"Oh, Rowena," said Prince Burnet gently. "I can see you are truly sorry for what you have done. Let us hope that my brother Trefoil is able to find your sister and bring her home safely to us all."

$\mathcal{P}$rincess Lisette had been carried a long way downstream and soon her leafboat began to sink. She managed to struggle ashore and found herself in a sheltered inlet. Here she rested in the shade of tangled vines which were weighed down with ripe berries upon which she fed.

Many tiny froglets who lived among the reeds came shyly out to talk to her, and as the days passed they became her little friends. They told her it was a good place to stay and that there was only one danger: sometimes a dragon would rise from the water to snap at flies — and froglets, if he could catch them!

"Perhaps he might even eat a fairy!" said one froglet. "If he should come you must run away and hide as we do."

The days slipped by, and then one warm sunny afternoon the princess was sitting near the water with her tiny friends when suddenly Prince Trefoil flew down and landed before her.

"At last, I have found you!" he cried joyfully. The princess, at first startled and then delighted to see him, was about to run into his arms when a huge dragon rose in a great rush of spray from the stream and lunged forwards.

The froglets leapt away in all directions. "Run, Lisette," yelled the prince as he drew his sword to protect her. But the dragon's long tail swept round and knocked him to the ground.

Lisette did not flee. She saw the dragon bend its neck and look down at the prince, and she thought it was about to devour him. She had no weapon to hand and no stones to throw, so she pulled off the magic armlet and flung it at the dragon's head.

The spinning armlet flashed in the sunlight,
and the dragon snapped at it and swallowed it whole. Then,
its magic spell began to work, and sapped him of his strength.
He fell back into the stream and sank slowly into its depths,
never to return.

The dragon's claw had wounded Prince Trefoil, but Princess Lisette made bandages of cobwebs and healing salves from streamside herbs. As he regained his strength, so too did she recover hers and she soon found that she could fly once more. At last, the day came for them to say goodbye to their froglet friends, and together they flew up the valley to the fern kingdom of King Azolla.

What cheers and rejoicing took place when they arrived! A huge feast was prepared to welcome them, and there it was announced that Princess Rowena would marry Prince Burnet, while Princess Lisette would marry her beloved Trefoil. In a moment of quiet, Rowena spoke sorrowfully to her sister of her wrong-doing, and begged for her forgiveness. Lisette lovingly forgave her, and together the two couples planned happily for their wedding.

A double wedding took place which was of such
magnificence that no-one in the entire valley
ever forgot it. Everyone in the fern kingdom
was invited, from the whole
royal family through to the humblest
mouse and honeybee.

The happy fairy couples flew
away to their new homes among
the foxgloves and meadowsweet.

Princess Rowena only used her gift
for the good of others — so the fairy folk
lived happily ever after.

And the dragon who had swallowed the armlet
lay spellbound at the bottom of the stream, never to
frighten the froglets again.